The Night Before St. Patrick's Day

enter

🍀
🍀
🍀
🍀

shiny→ treasure inside

Grosset & Dunlap

To elementary school teachers—my lucky charms!—N.W.
In memory of Pat Moyer.—A.W.

GROSSET & DUNLAP
Published by the Penguin Group
Penguin Group (USA) Inc., 375 Hudson Street, New York, New York 10014, USA
Penguin Group (Canada), 90 Eglinton Avenue East, Suite 700, Toronto, Ontario M4P 2Y3, Canada
(a division of Pearson Penguin Canada Inc.)
Penguin Books Ltd., 80 Strand, London WC2R 0RL, England
Penguin Group Ireland, 25 St. Stephen's Green, Dublin 2, Ireland
(a division of Penguin Books Ltd.)
Penguin Group (Australia), 250 Camberwell Road, Camberwell, Victoria 3124, Australia
(a division of Pearson Australia Group Pty. Ltd.)
Penguin Books India Pvt. Ltd., 11 Community Centre, Panchsheel Park, New Delhi—110 017, India
Penguin Group (NZ), 67 Apollo Drive, Rosedale, North Shore 0632, New Zealand
(a division of Pearson New Zealand Ltd.)
Penguin Books (South Africa) (Pty.) Ltd., 24 Sturdee Avenue,
Rosebank, Johannesburg 2196, South Africa

Penguin Books Ltd., Registered Offices:
80 Strand, London WC2R 0RL, England

Text copyright © 2009 by Natasha Wing. Illustrations copyright © 2009 by Amy Wummer. All rights reserved. Published by Grosset & Dunlap, a division of Penguin Young Readers Group, 345 Hudson Street, New York, New York 10014. GROSSET & DUNLAP and READING RAILROAD are trademarks of Penguin Group (USA) Inc. Printed in the U.S.A.

Library of Congress Control Number: 2008020699

ISBN 978-0-448-44852-7   10 9 8 7 6 5 4 3

The Night Before St. Patrick's Day

By Natasha Wing • Illustrated by Amy Wummer

Grosset & Dunlap

'Twas the night before St. Patrick's—

the day to wear green.

Not a creature was stirring,

except Tim and Maureen.

They decked out the den
from ceiling to floor
with streamers and rainbows
and shamrocks galore.

Later they carefully made traps
with gold charms and rings.

"I bet we catch a leprechaun.
They love shiny things."
For if they caught one—
so the legend told—
they'd find where he buried
his big pot of gold.

They set all the traps
'round the room with great care,
in hopes a wee Irishman
soon would be theirs.

enter

shiny→
treasure
inside

The children then nestled
all snug in their beds,
while visions of golden coins
danced in their heads.

"Happy St. Paddy's!" said Da
early the next morning.
Then he started to play
bagpipes without warning.

He huffed and he puffed
an old Irish song.

Mom dished out
green eggs

and sang loudly along.

When, from their bedroom,
there arose such a clatter,
the kids ran down the hallway
to see what was the matter.

And what to their wondering eyes
should appear . . .

. . . but a terrible mess.
A leprechaun was here!

"Be quiet," whispered Maureen.
"He's hiding somewhere.
When we find him, remember,
we must hold his stare."
For if you look away,
if you so much as blink,
leprechauns vanish,
quick as a wink.

The kids trailed muddy footprints
back and forth 'cross the floor . . .

which led them under Tim's bed
and past the closet door.

And then, inside a trap,
they heard someone giggling.
A real live leprechaun!
They both saw him wriggling.

His eyes—how they twinkled! His body so tiny!

His hand clasped a trinket so golden and shiny!
He was dressed in all green, from his head to his toes,
and he looked like a cobbler wearing fairy-sized clothes.

The children approached him,
staring straight in his eyes.
"Tell us where the gold is.
Don't be tricky—no lies!"

"I buried it under a rock,
smooth and hard.
It's marked with an X
right in your backyard."

But when the kids went outside
with their shovel and pick,

they instantly saw
it had been a big trick!